The Christmas Gift

Paradise Press, Inc.

The soldier told her what was in his heart. "I love you," he said. "Please, please, please come away with me and see the world."

"But this is our world. We can be together and safe right here. We don't need to go anywhere," she explained.

The soldier wasn't convinced. He wanted to see what life was like in the world outside the little shop, but he could not leave the ballerina behind.

"If I go without you, my heart will break," he said sadly.

The ballerina could not take that chance. At last she agreed to go.

The two said goodbye to all their friends and headed out to the shop. They got as far as the owner's quarters, when they heard a strange purring sound. It was his hungry cat!

The soldier and the ballerina quickly hid and waited. After a while, he gave up.

The ballerina tried to convince her friend to go back, but the soldier just shrugged. "Why, we haven't even gotten out of the house, yet," he said.

Together they made it through the parlor and out the mail slot in the front door.

But outside that door were more terrifying things waiting for them.

They dodged stray cats and dogs, trucks, cars, and people's feet.

They fled to a park with a pretty garden where they thought they'd be safe. But no sooner had they gotten to the park, when a big blackbird flew down and grabbed the ballerina in his beak. He flew up to a branch of a tall tree and dropped her in his nest.

The soldier heard the ballerina's cries for help and followed them. He found the tree, but had to figure out a way to climb up.

Looking down, he grabbed the little piece of rope that was looped around his belt, but it didn't reach very far.

Next, he tried to climb the tree, but he kept sliding down.

Calling up to the ballerina, he told her that he'd be right back. "I'm going for help! Don't be afraid!" he cried.

Then he ran as fast as he could to the toy shop.

He told the toy fire engine (with the longest ladder ever made) what had happened.

"Well," said the fire engine, "we can use my ladder to bring her down. Jump on and hold onto your hat!"

The soldier hopped onto the fire engine and took off followed by the cowboy doll on horseback, a wind-up penguin, and clown marionette.

When they got to the tree, the cowboy doll fastened a rope around the soldier's waist and held on.

The soldier stepped onto the ladder as the fire engine went to work. He raised it up higher and higher until it reached the branch.

"Yipee-i-o!" shouted the cowboy. "This is a real live adventure!"

At last, the soldier reached the nest and brought the ballerina down.

"Hurray!" The toys all cheered.

They rode back to the toy shop as fast as they could.

When they were safely back inside the shop, the ballerina hugged the wooden soldier.

Then she walked over to the music box, opened the top, and began to dance.

"It may not be much, but this is my Christmas gift to you," she told the soldier. "I wanted you to be the first one to see my new dance."

The soldier was so happy to be back safe and sound watching his ballerina dance, he knew that he would never leave home again.

"That's the best Christmas gift anyone ever gave me," he told her. "What a wonderful homecoming."

"Let's celebrate this and every Christmas together right here where we belong," she said, smiling and twirling on her toes.

One Christmas not so long ago, there was a magical toy shop in a cozy little town. After every busy day, when the shop was locked up tight, the toys and ornaments came to life.

Each night a wooden soldier watched as a ballerina ornament danced to her favorite song. A pretty little music box played the tune over and over again.

"Maybe tonight is the night I tell her," the soldier thought to himself.

But he didn't say a word that night or the next night or the night after that.

Then one special night, the wooden soldier decided he would work up the courage to tell the ballerina that he loved her. He wanted her to run away with him and see the world.

The ballerina stepped onto the stage of the puppet theater and began to dance. The soldier watched her from behind the curtain.

Suddenly he walked over to the music box and threw down the lid. "Stop! That's enough!" he cried.

"Why, whatever is the matter?" asked the ballerina.